W9-BKA-729

Stop Your Crowing, Kasimir!

Stop Your Crowing,
Kasimir!

by Ursel Scheffler

illustrations by Silke Brix-Henker

Carolrhoda Books, Inc./Minneapolis

"Just like a picture book!" That's what people would always say when they saw Katy feeding the hens in front of her old house.

And a picture-book life was just
what everyone dreamed of when they
moved into the new housing development on the outskirts of the city. Peace
and quiet and fresh country air. That
was what they all looked forward to.

Every morning when the rooster crowed, Katy got out of bed. She milked her two cows and the goat, fed the pigs and the hens, patted the dog and the cat, then made herself a nice cup of tea.

But one morning, chaos broke out in the barn. "Moo! Mooo! … Maah! Maaaaah! … Oink! Oiiiiink! … Cluck! Cluck, cluck, cluck, cluuuuuck! … Woof! … Meowww!"

The animals made such a racket that Katy jumped out of bed, terrified. "My goodness! It's broad daylight already! Why didn't the rooster wake me up?"

She soon discovered why when she went to the barn. Her poor rooster had died of old age. Katy quickly soothed the other animals. "We'll have to get a new rooster right away, that's for sure," she told them.

So that very Saturday, Katy got on her bicycle and pedaled to the market, just as she did every week, to sell her eggs and vegetables. But this time, Katy just couldn't seem to keep her mind on business. Three times she counted out the wrong change, and all because she kept hearing a rooster crowing in the distance. She could hardly wait until she could go and look for that rooster.

The rooster's voice could be heard all over the market. It led Katy straight to a farmer who was selling animals.

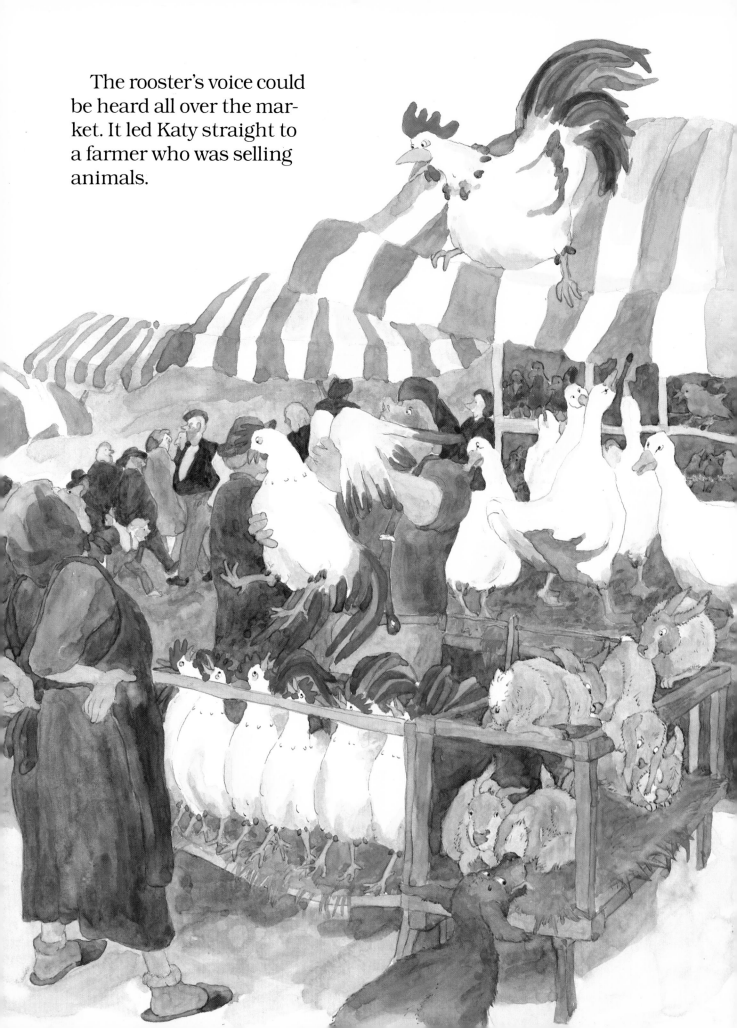

And there, on the roof of his market stall, Katy saw a huge, fat rooster. "That's him!" she exclaimed. "That's the one I want!"

"Kasimir? My market crier?" replied the farmer. "I need him myself. But look here—I've got lots more splendid roosters. All big and strong, fat and powerful!"

He lifted up one rooster after another, but Katy found fault with every one of them. The last one he showed her croaked wretchedly. "That one? With that rusty voice?" she demanded. "I need one with a crow that will get me out of bed in the morning. One just like Kasimir!"

"Oh, all right," sighed the farmer. "Take him!"

So Katy pedaled home happily with Kasimir right behind her.

Back at Katy's cottage, Kasimir felt right at home. Full of self-confidence, he strutted into the barn.

"Cluck, cluck, cluuuuck! Isn't he big!"

"Cluck, cluck, cluuuck! Isn't he strong!"

"Cluck, cluck, cluuuuck! Isn't he hand-some!" the hens cackled excitedly.

And once again Katy was
awakened on time each morning.
So everyone was happy....
Well, not *quite* everyone.

Mrs. Moaner, for one, was outraged. Every morning she was awakened by Kasimir's crowing. Finally, one morning when she could stand it no longer, she sat up in bed and screeched at her husband. "There's that terrible rooster crowing again! Doesn't it bother you at all?"

But Mr. Moaner was snoring away and, as usual, hadn't heard a thing. So Mrs. Moaner gave her husband a jab in the ribs. "Quiet! I want quiet!" she shouted.

When he finally woke up, the crowing began to annoy Mr. Moaner, too. "After all, we did move out to the country for some peace and quiet," he grumbled. "And now this! It's too much!"

The next Monday, Katy hauled the manure from her barn out to her little plot of land in the country, just as she did every Monday. And just as they did every Monday, the neighbors stopped and turned up their noses. "Such an awful stink!" they complained.

"That old house is an eyesore in our lovely area," Mr. Moaner said as he painted his fence.

"And then there's that awful rooster!" one neighbor complained. "There's not a single morning we can have a decent sleep! That creature should be done away with!"

"Steps have already been taken," Mrs. Moaner informed them with a mysterious look on her face. "Disturbing the peace every night—now *that's* a matter for the police!"

And while the neighbors went on making their nasty comments, Katy peacefully spread the manure on her little plot in the country. Now, spreading manure is tiring work, so when she finished, Katy washed up in the nearby stream, unwrapped her lunch, and sat down at the edge of the meadow near her barn where the quacking ducks were waiting for crumbs.

As always, Katy threw her
bread crusts to the ducks (she
couldn't bite them properly anyway)
and Kasimir found himself a fat earthworm.

The next day at 11 o'clock, much to Katy's surprise, the mailman rode right up to her kitchen window just as she was mixing the batter to make some pancakes for lunch. "Mail for me?" she asked in astonishment. She rarely received letters.

Eagerly she tore open the envelope but then turned pale as she read what the letter said:

Summons against Kasimir the rooster
on April 13 at 10 a.m.
Allegation: Nightly disturbance of the peace
The District Court.

"Oh dear," said Katy as she lovingly stroked Kasimir's neck. "I'm so upset. But the law is the law. We'll have to go to court!"

So the next morning, she packed a basket full of chicken feed, tucked Kasimir under her arm, and set off for the local courthouse. Cackling with excitement, the hens scampered after Katy and Kasimir.

The trial took place in a big room in the courthouse. First the witnesses were questioned. Then Kasimir had his say. He spoke out with such a noisy "Cock-a-doodle-doo!" that the startled judges covered their ears. The neighbors looked at each other in triumph.

"You can hear for yourselves what a loud voice he has," Mr. Moaner grumbled.

When Katy looked around at her neighbors' sneering faces, she suddenly couldn't stand it in the courtroom any longer. So she ran outside into the hallway and sat on a bench with her hens to wait for a decision.

Katy could hear her heart thumping. What will the court order? she wondered.

Finally the judges made their decision.
"Crowing is banned!" the chief judge ordered.
"Or the rooster must go!"

The neighbors gloated when he
said that. It was just what they wanted to hear.

At home that evening, Katy put all the hens into the barn and gave them fresh water. She looked anxiously at Kasimir and sighed. "What am I going to do with you now that you can't crow?" She sat brooding  in the chicken coop until midnight.

At last, Katy had a brilliant idea. She fetched a gauze bandage and wrapped it tightly around Kasimir's beak.

"There," she said. "That ought to keep you from crowing in the morning." Relieved, Katy went to bed.

But a rooster like Kasimir doesn't give in to a crowing ban! First he scraped his beak on the hen trestle, then he fluttered wildly around the chicken coop—he even worked on the bandage with his claws. Soon it began to loosen, and with the help of the clamoring hens, the job was finally done!

When the sun came up the next morning, Kasimir crowed even louder than usual.

Officer Caraway soon arrived to warn Katy. "This can't go on!" he said. "Nobody can sleep anymore in the morning because your rooster crows so loudly. Not even me. I'm awakened by everyone calling me to complain! That rooster has to go!"

"Not on your life!" said Katy. "I need him."

"Then I'll grab that noisy troublemaker!" shouted Officer Caraway. And huffing with rage, he ran after Kasimir.

But no policeman in the world is as fast as Kasimir. Officer Caraway tripped over a sack of potatoes. And Kasimir? Why, he flew up to the roof and crowed cheerfully.

Officer Caraway shouted, "You wait! The next time I'll come with the whole fire department!"

And as she watched Officer Caraway walk off in a huff, Katy thought, "I can't stand it here any longer! I'll sell my cottage and move away!"

So the next morning, Katy packed all her belongings and drove out to her farm in the country. "You'll see what a cozy life it'll be in the old barn," she told her animals.

Back in the housing development, Katy's neighbors were delighted. At last there would be peace and quiet.

The very next morning, Mrs. Moaner was jerked out of her sleep at dawn. "What is that noise?" she cried as she ran to the window. A steam roller was rumbling outside. Katy's old house was being remodeled.

"Construction machines!" wailed Mrs. Moaner.

"That's what you get!" grumbled Mr. Moaner as he turned onto his other side.

"It'll only last for a short while," Mrs. Moaner told him. "We'll go on vacation for a few days. When we come back, the house will be finished."

When the Moaners returned from their vacation, they were in a cheerful mood. The machines had disappeared, and Katy's old house was freshly painted.

"There you are. I was right!" said Mrs. Moaner happily. She set the table for the evening meal, which was roast chicken, their favorite dish.

Suddenly they heard droning and roaring in the distance. Closer and closer it came. Soon the sounds of engines, loud horns blowing, and screeching brakes were right outside their window.

"What—what's that now?" Mr. Moaner cried out, startled. "Noisy traffic? Here? At this time of night?" He nearly choked on his last mouthful of chicken.

"Nightly disturbance of the peace!" Mrs. Moaner gasped. "This is a matter for the police!" So once again she called Officer Caraway.

"Haven't you heard?" asked Officer Caraway. "The new disco opens tonight." And for the first time in her life, Mrs. Moaner was speechless.

Meanwhile, Katy and her animals had settled into her old farm in the country. Now, each evening as they watch the sun go down on the far side of the meadow, Katy sighs in relief. "Finally, at last, we have some peace and quiet!"

Translated from the German by Andrea Kunze-Galt.

This edition first published 1988 by Carolrhoda Books, Inc.
Original edition copyright © 1986 by Annette Betz Verlag
im Verlag Carl Ueberreuter, Vienna and Munich, under the title
KRÄHVERBOT FÜR KASIMIR.
All English-language rights reserved by Carolrhoda Books, Inc.
Printed in Austria and bound in the United States of America.

Library of Congress Cataloging-in-Publication Data

Scheffler, Ursel.
  Stop your crowing, Kasimir!

  Translation of: Krähverbot für Kasimir.
  Summary: Katy's neighbors appeal to the
authorities to silence her extremely loud
rooster, but the final result is very different
from what they had in mind.
  [1. Roosters—Fiction. 2. Neighborliness—
Fiction] I. Brix-Henker, Silke, ill. II. Title.
PZ7.S3425St 1988   [E]   87-9319
ISBN 0-87614-323-0 (lib. bdg.)

1 2 3 4 5 6 7 8 9 10 98 97 96 95 94 93 92 91 90 89 88